BUSH AND BEYOND

This edition first published in 2018 by
FREMANTLE PRESS
25 Quarry Street, Fremantle 6160
Western Australia
www.fremantlepress.com.au

Bush Secrets was first published as an individual title in 2009; *Barlay!*
was first published as an individual title in 2010; *Yippee! Summer
Holidays* was first published as an individual title in 2012 *Lucky Thamu*
was first published as an individual title in 2014.

Cover design and cover illustration by traceygibbs.com.au.
Printed by McPherson's Printing Group, Australia.

National Library of Australia Cataloguing-in-publication data available.

ISBN 9781925591132 (pbk)

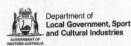

Department of
**Local Government, Sport
and Cultural Industries**
GOVERNMENT OF
WESTERN AUSTRALIA

Fremantle Press is supported by the State Government through
the Department of Local Government, Sport and Cultural Industries

BUSH AND BEYOND

STORIES FROM COUNTRY

TJALAMINU MIA
JESSICA LISTER
CHERYL KICKETT-TUCKER
JAYLON TUCKER

FREMANTLE PRESS

CONTENTS

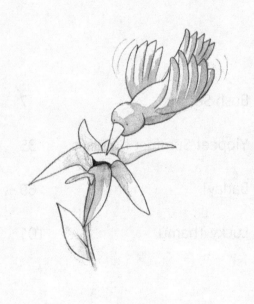

Bush Secrets

TJALAMINU MIA
AND
JESSICA LISTER

GREEN COUNTRY

I've got a secret and I'm so excited!

Actually, I've got two secrets and that makes me feel really happy inside.

'What are you grinning at, Debbie?' my brother Billy asks.

'Nothing.' I don't want him guessing my secrets.

'You've got a secret, haven't you?'

'No I haven't.'

'Yes you have! I can tell! What is it, Debbie?'

'I'm not telling you, Billy!'

He throws a honky nut at me. 'Tell me!'

'No!'

He throws another nut. 'Well, I've got a secret too!'

'What is it then?'

'My special tree is bigger than yours!' Billy looks sly. 'I told you my secret Debbie, now you have to tell me yours!'

I laugh. 'That's not a secret, that's a fib. My special tree is much bigger than yours!'

Billy picks up a big honky nut and flings it at me. It hits my arm and really stings. Boy, am I mad! I yell, 'Actually I have two secrets and I'm not going to tell you about them now!'

'Keep your silly secrets then!' he says, storming off.

I know where he's going, back to the house to tell Mum I've been mean to him. Then I'll get into trouble. Why are little brothers so annoying?

I slump down under my favourite tree, the one that's taller than Billy's, and look out over the bush. I'm a Nyungar girl and I live in green country. At least, that's what some people call it. In green country there are lots of birds and animals and creeks and rivers, but most of all there are trees. Tall trees, short trees, skinny trees and fat ones too. They're all different from each other, with different leaves, trunks and bark. Knobbly nuts grow on their branches and these nuts turn into pretty coloured flowers, which smell really nice. When the bees buzz around the flowers, Billy and I have to be careful we don't get stung. Birds and possums make their homes in the trees. I love climbing to the very top of my tree like a possum and looking out over the land to the blue coloured hills in the distance. High in the sky, no one can see me. It is my own personal hide out.

I've invented a secret name for my favourite tree. It's made up of three words – gorgeous, gem and Christmas. I put them all

together and made Gorgemas. Mum agrees
that my tree is the best tree in the world. She
says it's like a beautiful gem. At Christmas
time Mum helps me decorate Gorgemas. We
make paper cut outs of animals and stick bits
of coloured wool on them. They are lovely, but
the shiny string of bells and stars Mum makes
out of silver chocolate paper looks the best.
I'm the only one who knows my tree's name.
That's my first secret. But my second secret is
even bigger. Gorgemas has a bird's nest with
three eggs hidden in a hollow in the trunk

near the very top. The eggs are white with little brown specks.

I don't want to tell Billy my secrets because I don't think he really understands what a secret is. Besides, Mum told us she is expecting a visitor, and I don't want Billy blabbing my special secrets to just anyone.

SURPRISE!

'Come on you kids!' Mum calls after lunch.
'It's time to go to the train station.'

We're expecting a parcel from our
grandparents, Nana and Dada Keen, who live
in the city with all our uncles and aunties. Billy is
getting new boots and I'm getting a new dress.
We don't see our grandparents very often, so
we're excited about the parcel arriving. There
might be a letter in it too, with all the family
news from Perth.

As we pull into the station we can hear
the train whistle blowing and see smoke rising
above the tree tops in the distance. We wait

on the platform. It's always exciting when the train arrives, especially when you're expecting a present.

'Stop jumping about!' Mum growls at us. 'You might fall onto the tracks and get squashed, then neither of you will be wearing those new clothes!'

When the train pulls in we move down the platform towards the guard's van, where they store all the parcels. The guard loads everything onto a trolley and rolls it onto the platform. Mum picks out the parcel that belongs to us then signs the goods form to say it's been delivered safely.

'I can't wait to get home and see my new dress!' I tell Mum.

'I hope my boots are the right size,' says Billy.

The platform is crowded with people now. All the passengers from Perth have left the train.

Mum smiles at us and says, 'I wonder who that is walking towards us?'

We look in the direction she's pointing and can't believe our eyes. Coming towards us is a short man carrying a small suitcase. His hat is tilted to one side of his head and there's a big grin on his face. It's Dada Keen!

'Surprise!' he calls out to us.

We hug him so hard we nearly knock him over.

'So you're the visitor Mum was expecting!' I giggle. 'She kept it a big secret!'

Dada Keen and Mum look at each other and laugh.

I'm really happy. It's the best surprise Billy and I have had in a long time.

GORGEMAS

Dada Keen hasn't always lived in the city. He grew up in the bush. We love it when he visits because he has lots of interesting stories to tell us about the birds and plants and animals.

The next morning after breakfast I tell him, 'I've got a secret to show you.'

'Secrets are special things, Debbie,' he replies. 'Are you sure you want to share your secret with me?'

I grin. 'Actually, I've got two secrets. And yes, I'm sure.'

I wait until Billy is doing his jobs for Mum, then I take Dada Keen out to meet Gorgemas.

'What a good name for such a beautiful tree,' he says.

When I tell him about the bird's nest with the speckled eggs tucked away at the top he nods. 'The birds must like your tree too, because they've built their nest in it. You're very lucky to have two special secrets.'

'Thank you, Dada Keen.'

Dada Keen bends down and whispers. 'I've

got a secret too Debbie – a very important one. If I share it with you, will you keep it safe and not tell anyone?'

'Of course I will! What is it?'

Just then a voice calls loudly, 'Hey Debbie, what are you doing?' Billy comes running up the hill to join us.

Dada Keen waves to him, then winks at me, 'Don't worry Debbie, I won't tell anyone your secrets. And tomorrow I'll show you something very special. It will be a long walk though, so you'll need to have a good sleep tonight.'

Billy rushes up and shows Dada Keen some of the honky nuts lying near his tree. I notice he doesn't say he sometimes throws them at me!

Will Dada Keen bring Billy with us when we go bushwalking tomorrow? I hope not. I've never had a special outing on my own with Dada Keen. It would be lovely if, for once, it could just be the two of us.

I cross my fingers and make a wish. Please let me go bushwalking with Dada Keen alone tomorrow.

Will my wish come true?

BUSHWALKING

The next day Mum bakes Dada Keen scones
with jam and cream for morning tea.

'Delicious!' he says. 'They don't make
scones like these in the city.'

Mum smiles. She likes it when people
enjoy her cooking. Then she winks at me.
Something is going on – but what?

'Billy,' Mum says, 'I have to go into town to
buy a few things. Do you want to come along?'

Billy looks at me and Dada Keen. I can see
he's trying to decide which will be the most
fun, staying on the farm or going with Mum.

Dada Keen yawns. 'My train journey tired

me out, I think I might need a little nap today.'

'I'll come, Mum!' Billy says.

After they leave, Dada Keen fills a billycan with clean water and his canvas bag with the sandwiches Mum made for our lunch. She didn't want Billy to see them, so she hid them at the very back of the fridge behind a bowl of potato salad. We head off across one of the big sheep paddocks, then duck under the wire fence at the end of it and disappear into the bush. It'd be easy to get lost because there's more than one bush track to follow, but Dada Keen knows which path to take.

'Here Debbie,' he says. 'Tie four little knots at the end of each of these handkerchiefs, then pour some water over them from the billycan. They'll keep our heads cool when we're walking through the bush.'

I feel a bit silly with a wet handkerchief on my head, but it's a hot day and it does make me cooler.

We walk for a long time, so long that
I'm wondering if we'll ever get there, when
Dada Keen stops and says, 'You stay here for a
moment Debbie, I just want to check around
a bit and make sure we're in exactly the right
spot.'

All of a sudden I'm alone. It's scary. I hope
a snake doesn't slither by. I stand there for
ages, then I hear a voice calling, 'Coo-ee!
Coo-ee!'

I stand very still and listen again.

'Coo-ee!'

It's Dada Keen!

I call back 'Coo-ee! Coo-ee!' just like he taught me when I was small.

Dada Keen comes out of the bush behind me and smiles. 'That's good, you did the right thing Debbie. You called back twice and you didn't wander off. Now I'm going to show you something special, so close your eyes and take my hand.'

Dada Keen leads me deeper and deeper into the bush. Soon I can hear the bubbling sound of running water.

Where are we?

BUSH PERFUME

'We've arrived!' Dada Keen says. 'You can
open your eyes now.'

'Oh!' I gasp.

Spread out before us is a carpet of
wildflowers. Even my favourite ones are there,
the donkey and spider orchids. The water from
the creek has made them lush and thick. The
perfume of the many different flowers blends
with the smell of the eucalyptus trees and fills
the air.

Dada Keen breathes deeply. 'It's a
wonderful smell, isn't it?'

I breathe deeply too. 'It's bush perfume.'

'I knew you'd like it Debbie, you have a heart for the bush.'

We stand there together, not saying anything, just thinking about how lovely it is.

Then on the ground I notice creepers with blue and pink and yellow flowers. Some of them are wound together, one over the other.

'Dada Keen,' I say in surprise, 'look at the colours of those flowers and the way the plants are woven together! They're just like a double rainbow. Whenever Billy and I see a double rainbow in the sky we always make a wish.'

Dada Keen smiles. 'I wondered when you'd notice them. They're very special, Debbie. But they're so delicate that if you handle them roughly they will shrivel up and die.'

'Earth rainbow,' I say in awe. It's amazing!

'When the sun comes out after it's rained, the plants sparkle like diamonds. When the water drips off them it looks like small droplets of rainbow are sinking back into the earth.'

'That's good, isn't it?'

'Yes, it's very good for the land. You see, these little rainbow plants that lie over the earth are just like the big rainbows in the sky. When I see them, they make me feel happy.'

'Me too,' I sigh. 'Is this a secret place Dada Keen?'

He nods. 'It sure is! This place and these plants are two of my special secrets, just like Gorgemas and the nest with the speckled eggs are yours. I don't tell many people because I want to keep this spot safe. But now that I've shared them with you Debbie, will you keep my secrets?'

KEEPING SECRETS

I give Dada Keen a big hug. 'Of course I will.
I'll help you to protect this place, too. Thank
you for showing it to me.'

'Come on Debbie, let's sit under this
shady gum and have our lunch. We can look
at the wildflowers while we're eating.'

It's nice watching the bees buzzing around
the flowers and the tiny birds hovering over
them and sticking their little beaks into the
petals.

'Do they want to eat the flowers?' I ask.

He laughs. 'The birds are like us. They
enjoy sweet things too and the flower nectar

is very sweet.'

'Bush lollies for the birds?'

'That's right! It's a wonderful treat that nature provides for them.'

After we finish our sandwiches it's time

to leave. I don't want to go. This is such a
beautiful place I could stay here forever.

'Does Mum know about the earth
rainbows, Dada Keen?' I ask, as we make our
way back through the bush.

'Yes, I showed them to her when she was
a little girl too. It's a secret she's kept all her
life.'

'What about Billy? Will you bring him here
one day?'

'Billy is very young, Debbie. Something
tells me he doesn't know how to keep a
secret yet. Perhaps when he's a bit older, we
can all come out here together. But that's
only when Billy learns there are some secrets
which are important to keep.'

As we head towards home, I feel very
proud Dada Keen has shared his secrets with
me. I never imagined a secret could be so
important, but this one is. When something
really special needs protecting, like my bird's

nest or Dada Keen's rainbow plants, then the only way to keep it safe is to keep that secret close to your heart.

Yippee! Summer Holidays

TJALAMINU MIA

AND

JESSICA LISTER

SUMMER HOLIDAYS

'Wake up, wake up, Debbie!' Billy yells with delight as he runs into my bedroom. 'Yippee, yippee, we don't have school today, it's the holidays!'

Yippee is Billy's favourite word and I'm getting sick of hearing it.

'Go away, Billy, it's still dark outside. I want to sleep some more.' Billy gets up so early on the holidays!

When I wake up next the sun is warm on my face and this makes me smile. I quickly jump out of bed to look outside.

The sun is shining and the sky is blue. There is just one white fluffy cloud floating towards the purple hills in the distance. It is a perfect day to start the summer holidays.

These holidays are going to be the best ever because my grandfather Dada Keen is coming to visit us. I love it when Dada Keen visits us because he knows lots of special places in the bush, and sometimes he takes me to see them.

As I run to join my mum and Billy for breakfast, I think — I love living in the bush and I love the summer holidays.

DADA KEEN'S LETTER

'Debbie, can you and Billy go and see if the
mail has arrived?' Mum asks.

We are hoping to get a letter from our
grandfather letting us know when he will
arrive. *Please*, I silently pray — *let there be a
letter from Dada Keen.*

'Yippee, yippee,' yells Billy. 'We've got the
letter!' Billy runs all the way back to the house
to give it to Mum.

'I can come to visit you for two weeks.
I arrive on next Friday morning's train from
Perth,' Dada Keen writes in his letter. 'Tell
Debbie and Billy I have won some money in
Lotto, so the prize for the next tyre race will

be five dollars.'

Billy and I are so excited. We both yell as we run outside to get our tyres to practise.

'I'm going to win, I'm going to win.'

'No you're not, I am!'

RACING TYRES

Billy and I play lots of games, like hopscotch
and marbles, but the game we like best of all
is racing tyres. Our grandfather showed us
how to play the last time he stayed.

We race our old car tyres down the hill
to the fence at the bottom of the sheep
paddock. The first one there is the winner, but
you have to keep your tyre with you.

When Billy and I race our tyres, we stand
them up and lean them against the side of our
legs so they don't fall down. We walk slowly
and push the tyres gently with our hands.

Dada Keen says it's all about rhythm. He

says we have to make our tyres move at the
same time we do.

It gets hard though when we start running.
As we pick up speed so do our tyres! Running
in a straight line down the hill isn't easy. If we

don't keep up with our tyres, they roll away by themselves.

I love this game because when you run fast the wind blows in your face and makes your eyes water and your cheeks tingle. My long hair blows up into the air. Billy always laughs at me. He says I look funny.

Racing tyres is so much fun!

Our racing tyres are black, but Billy has a yellow line down the middle of his and I have a red line on mine. I painted yellow flames around my red line and Billy got angry. He said the flames made my tyre go faster than his.

'Why has Debbie got flames on her tyre and I haven't?' Billy whined to our grandfather, so Dada Keen painted flames on his tyre too. Billy is such a cry-baby sometimes.

I can't wait for Dada Keen to arrive. Only one more sleep, and he'll be here!

COLOURED STREAMERS

After we pick up Dada Keen from the train station, the first thing he does is check our tyres to see if they need fixing.

Then Dada Keen puts two big bolt screws on each side of the hole in our tyres and ties bunches of long crepe paper streamers to the bolts. He puts red streamers on Billy's tyre and yellow streamers on mine.

Dada Keen doesn't say anything while he's doing this. He just looks at us and smiles, so we smile too.

'Dada Keen, why are you doing that to our tyres?' Billy asks eventually. Billy always asks questions when he's not supposed to!

'Just be patient Billy, you'll soon see,' our grandfather replies.

Billy and I look at each other — we are very curious now. I wonder what my grandfather is up to?

Then Dada Keen asks Billy to go to the shed and bring him the old wooden wheelbarrow. He puts our tyres in the wheelbarrow and pushes them to the starting line for our race.

RUSTY OLD WINDMILL

There is an old rusty windmill in the paddock
near our house. It pumps water from the dam
to the sheep troughs so they have water to
drink.

'I'll check for rocks on the racetrack. You
kids keep an eye on the windmill,' says our
grandfather.

'Why Dada Keen?' I ask.

'When the wind starts to blow, the
windmill will change course and that's when
we start the race,' he replies.

The windmill is very tall, even taller than
my favourite tree Gorgemas. Billy and I are
allowed to climb our trees but not the windmill.

Mum says it is too dangerous. If you climbed
the ladder to the top and the wind changed
direction, you would be in big trouble. It has
rusty old blades and if you weren't quick
enough to duck under the blades, you could

get your head cut off.

The windmill has changed direction now and its blades are spinning around and around very fast. The wind is blowing really strongly and our coloured streamers fly high into the air. They look so cool, just like real flames!

THE RACE

Billy and I are very excited and look at each other nervously. Dada Keen makes a line in the dirt by dragging the heel of his old workboot along the ground. Billy and I step up to the mark. We look at each other, excited and nervous at the same time.

'On your marks! Get ready! GO!' Dada Keen shouts, and Billy and I start racing our tyres down the hill.

As we run faster and faster, our tyres roll faster and faster, too!

Dada Keen is right, our tyres look great as they race down the hill. The coloured streamers blow in the wind like blazing red

and yellow flames.

'I'm the winner, I won the race,' I yell over my shoulder as I reach the fence first. Then I see Billy's tyre roll into the fence by itself. My little brother is crying. He tripped and fell when his tyre rolled too fast and he couldn't keep up with it.

'It's not fair Debbie, you can run much faster than me,' he sobs.

'Don't be a baby Billy,' I say as I help him up. 'If you stop crying, I'll share the five dollar prize with you.'

Billy stops crying and smiles. He is my happy but annoying little brother again!

When we get back to the house, Billy runs in first to tell Mum about the tyre race.

Dada Keen gives me a big hug. 'Debbie, you're a good sister to Billy. I have a special reward for you for being nice to him.'

'What is it Dada Keen?'

'I'll show you tomorrow,' he says with a grin.

OUR CAMPFIRE

That night, Billy and I help Dada Keen build a campfire to roast marshmallows.

'I like campfires,' Billy says, as Dada Keen puts more wood on the fire. The yellow and red flames shoot up into the night sky looking just like the flames on our racing tyres.

We have lots of laughs around the campfire and Dada Keen tells us some great stories. The best story is about a waterhole.

'When I was a young boy, I walked across the paddocks into the bush not far from here to a waterhole where all the animals and birds went everyday for a drink of water.'

My little brother doesn't hear about the

waterhole because he has fallen asleep. I like
it when Billy falls asleep and Dada Keen and
I are left alone at the campfire. He tells me
some really good stories then, stories that he
hasn't told anyone else.

'Can you take me to the waterhole Dada Keen?' I ask.

'Yes, Debbie, I will — as your reward for being kind to your brother.'

I go to sleep that night feeling really happy.

YONGA'S BUSH TRACK

Dada Keen and I set out early the next morning.

'Debbie, have I told you the Nyungar word for kangaroo?' Dada Keen asks as we walk along.

'No, Dada Keen.'

'Well, we call kangaroos *yonga*,' he says as he writes the word in the sand with a big stick.

'Yonga,' I repeat slowly.

'This track we're on is called yonga's bush track. We're going to follow it to the waterhole. See the marks on the track? They're yonga's footprints.'

We bend down to have a closer look. Dada

Keen traces the outline of yonga's footprint with his finger and he explains why yonga's marks are so deep in the ground.

'Yonga has powerful legs and feet that he uses to hop. He only has three toes on each foot and the middle toe is the biggest. This big toe has a very sharp claw at the end of it. It helps him to grip the ground when he hops or when he wants to stop.'

'Yonga's footprints are really big, Dada Keen.'

'Yes, Debbie, they are, and you must never get too close to a bush kangaroo. If they get frightened, they might kick their legs and feet out and cut you with their sharp toe claw.'

THE WATERHOLE

'Not too much further to go now, we're nearly there,' my grandfather says as we reach the bottom of the hill.

Dada Keen and I have walked a long way through the bush. We climbed over a hill of huge rocks. And we passed through a stand of gum trees with sweet-smelling red blossoms.

Suddenly we come to the waterhole.

'Oh, what a lovely place!' I gasp.

It is very quiet except for a frog croaking. The waterhole is big and round and the water is dark brown. Dada Keen says all the gum leaves falling into the water make it this colour. He says they also make the water taste like eucalyptus.

There are some trees growing in the waterhole with pretty yellow flowers on them. The trees' bark looks like paper. Dada Keen says these trees are called paperbarks and they sometimes grow around waterholes.

'Dada Keen, where does the water come from?'

'There are special places where water is stored underground. But sometimes, a hole appears in the earth and water escapes. When this happens, the water fills up a place in the bush like here, and makes a waterhole,' answers Dada Keen. 'My grandfather told me this water is called sweet water because it is fresh and you can drink it.'

'Are there Nyungar words for water and waterhole Dada Keen?'

'Yes, Debbie. The Nyungar word for fresh water is *kep*, and waterhole is *kep boordja*.'

Wow, I have learnt three Nyungar words

today — yonga (kangaroo) kep (water) and kep boordja (waterhole). I will have to write them in my diary when I get home so I don't forget them.

'Dada Keen,' I ask, 'Why doesn't this water dry up in the summer like other water does?'

'This water comes from a special underground river that is protected from the sun,' my grandfather replies.

'Do all the birds and animals know about it?' I ask as I splash my fingers in the brown water.

'Birds and animals can smell fresh water from a long way off. When they need a drink they come here, and when there's a bushfire they come too, to stay safe. There are lots of plants and other living things that depend on the waterhole too.'

'What do you mean?' I ask as I look around.

My grandfather smiles at me and says, 'Look closely at the waterhole Debbie and tell me what you see.'

BUSH BALANCE

I describe everything I see. There are little green birds putting their beaks in the yellow flowers, eating the nectar. There is a black and yellow spider in its web and a green frog sitting on a log. And a gecko is crawling on the paperbark tree.

I move closer to the waterhole to see what else I can spy.

There are bubbles rising in the water. I wonder what is making them. Maybe it's a freshwater turtle? There are ants floating on top of a leaf in the water, and a dragonfly about to land on a stick.

I look around the waterhole one more

time, just to make sure I don't
leave anything out. There are
the trees and flowers, the
grasses and reeds, and all the
little insects too, like the beetles,
the bees and the pretty orange
and black butterflies.

'Very good, Debbie,' Dada Keen says, when
I finish. 'You really like the bush, don't you? It
is good to understand all the many things that
live and grow here. Everything works together,
a bit like a machine, and this keeps balance in
the place. You need to remember, Debbie —
balance in the bush is very important.'

'What do you mean, Dada Keen?'

'Well Debbie, everything that lives at
the waterhole is like a big family and the
waterhole is like their home, just like our
family and our home. When you and Billy help
each other and your mum, this keeps things
running smoothly,' my grandfather replies.

'Is this how the waterhole works too?'

'Yes, it's all about teamwork and balance. All the animals, birds and insects at the waterhole have a job to do. If they do their jobs, they help the water to stay fresh and there will be plenty of food for everyone to eat.'

As I look around the waterhole again I decide from now on, I'm going to help my mum around the house more and look after my little brother better.

'Debbie, let's sit on this old log for a little rest before we start our walk back home,' Dada Keen suggests.

YONGA SURPRISE

It is nice sitting with my grandfather in the bush. It is really quiet and peaceful.

Suddenly we hear a loud noise. I have never heard a sound like it before. The strange noise is getting louder and closer. It seems like the noise is coming towards us.

'Don't be afraid Debbie, just sit still for a moment,' Dada Keen says quietly as I look around nervously.

Thud, thud, thud. What can it be?

'Look, look, Dada Keen, it's yonga!' I yell, as a kangaroo hops past us through the bush.

'He was coming for a drink,' Dada Keen replies. 'He will return when we leave.'

It was good to see a kangaroo near the waterhole because we didn't see any along yonga's bush track.

'He was a big kangaroo Dada Keen, does he live at the waterhole too?' I ask.

'No Debbie, he doesn't. But he and other kangaroos come here every day to drink the fresh water and eat the green bush grasses.'

'There are many more things that live around the waterhole Debbie and some of them only come out at night. I'll tell you about them on the way home.'

As we walk back, I listen to my grandfather talk about all the other animals and insects that come to the waterhole at night. I never realised that so many things depended on the waterhole or that everything worked together like a big team-machine.

DADA KEEN'S NEXT VISIT

It has been a week since Dada Keen caught the train back to Perth. Billy and I are feeling sad because we didn't want him to go home. We are sitting in our favourite trees when we hear Mum.

'Stop moping you kids and come sit at the table,' Mum calls. She cuts two big slices of chocolate cake for us. She calls her cakes 'cheer-up' food and Billy and I soon cheer-up because the cake is so yummy!

'Debbie, I know you and Billy miss your grandfather, but don't be sad because he is visiting us again at Easter.'

'Yippee, yippee!' Billy screams as he runs

outside to get his tyre to practise.

I feel much better now, too. I'm happy because Dada Keen is coming again. I can't wait. He can help me find some really good hiding places for my Easter eggs. Billy will never find them!

Barlay!

CHERYL KICKETT-TUCKER

NAN'S STORY

Sarah and her brothers, Jay and Rene, lived
with their parents and Nan in a white house
with a red roof. The house sat high in the hills
on the Darling scarp, nestled amongst the
tall white gum trees. Many birds made their
homes in the trees and Sarah loved to listen
to them, and watch the bush animals eat and
play. She was a Noongar girl, so for her family
the bush was a spiritual place where people
could learn many special things.

One hot summer's night, just as the sun
was setting, Nan called Sarah and her brothers
out onto the back porch to tell them a story.
Sarah had a feeling the story was going to be

scary and important — and she was right.

Nan's twinkling brown eyes grew serious as the shadows deepened in the yard. 'This is the story of the *woordatj*,' she said softly.

'Nan, why are you whispering?' Sarah asked.

'The *woordatj* doesn't like to be disturbed. I don't want to wake him up in case he gets angry. Now, sit still and listen carefully.'

THE WOORDATJ

'The *woordatj* is short, but he has a long chin,
long arms with long fingers and long legs too,
only he walks bent over like an old man. He
is really hairy — hairy from his fingers and his
toes all the way up to his head and his nose.
The *woordatj* doesn't like to show himself
off to people, but that doesn't mean he's not
watching. If he's close by, you might just see
the red of his eyes.'

Is he close by now? Sarah wondered,
staring nervously into the dark garden. She
glanced at Rene, who was frowning. She
thought Rene wouldn't like to see him either.
But Jay, who was the oldest, just grinned and

tried to look tough.

'The *woordatj* is always around us. He is part of nature, so he is in contact with all living things.

'He talks with the trees, animals and birds like *chitty chitty* (willy wagtail), *koolbardi* (magpie), *djakal-ngakal* (galah) and *doornart* (parrot). But he likes to stay hidden.'

'Where does the *woordatj* live, Nan?' asked Sarah.

'There is a cave at Rocky Pool, tucked away next to a big shady old *wornt* (gum tree). The inside of the cave is a little wet, so it's a chilly, dark place. The *woordatj* camps there.'

'Now,' Nan continued, her voice becoming even softer, 'there is something very important you need to know about the *woordatj*. One of his jobs is to make sure children behave themselves and listen to the wise things their Elders tell them. If you don't ...'

Nan's voice trailed off.

'Then what, Nan?' asked Sarah quickly.

'Then at *kedalak* (sunset) the *woordatj* comes with an old sugar bag to look for naughty *koolongka* (children). So — *barlay!* (watch out!)'

A loud laugh rang out, startling them all. Sarah and her brothers jumped in fright.

Nan chuckled. 'It's only a *kaa kaa*. But I think that kookaburra is telling us it's time to go inside.'

A SURPRISE

'Would you like some pancakes?' Nan asked cheerfully, the next morning.

'Thanks, Nan. They look great!' Sarah reached for the honey to drizzle over them. 'What are we doing today?'

'It's such a lovely sunny day, why don't we go to Rocky Pool for a picnic?'

Sarah almost choked on her pancake. 'But that's where the *woordatj* lives!'

Nan smiled. 'We'll be back before *kedalak*. Everything will be fine as long as we head home while the sun's still up.'

Sarah's pushed her pancakes away. She

didn't feel like eating anymore. Jay and Rene laughed.

'Aren't you even a little bit scared?' Sarah asked her brothers.

'We're boys!' Jay said. 'We aren't scared of a short hairy creature with long arms!'

'And we can run fast if the *woordatj* comes close,' said Rene.

'Besides,' bragged Jay, 'I'm too tall to fit into a sugar bag!'

Nan frowned. 'The *woordatj* is a magical creature. He could shrink you two and bundle you up just like that!'

Jay whispered to Rene, 'Do you think Nan is just telling us a made up story about the *woordatj* to scare us?'

'Like a fairy tale, you mean? Maybe.'

Sarah sighed. Her brothers were silly sometimes, but they wouldn't listen to her. She just hoped they'd behave themselves at

Rocky Pool. Sarah decided she'd stay close to Nan, just in case anything went wrong. She wouldn't be able to have fun if she was worrying about the *woordatj*.

STAYING CLOSE

Rocky Pool was in the Kuljak National Park and it was the best place to be on a hot summer's day. The cool fresh water of the swimming hole was surrounded by a circle of large granite rocks. Sarah had never forgotten what Nan had told her about them: 'The rocks are old spirits. They look after the area and keep the *kep wari* (pool water) safe for everyone to use.'

Sometimes the water overflowed from the swimming hole and spilled down the side of the hill to form a bright, bubbling stream at the bottom. Here there was a small wooden bridge and Sarah loved to sit nearby and watch the noisy galahs and parrots, perched among the red and yellow flowers of the gum trees, talking heir heads off. Rocky Pool was a beautiful place during the day, but it was spooky at night. Sarah shivered, just thinking about it. When the sun began to set, odd shapes and shadows appeared across the land and the colours of the rock walls, crevices and small caves in the area changed. Nan had names for all the deep shades like *mirda* for red and *moorn* for black. Sarah felt glad her family always left before sunset. What would happen if they didn't?

ROCKY POOL

'We're here!' Dad sang out, pulling into the car park.

Jay and Rene flung open their doors and leapt out.

'Don't go any further than the bridge!' Mum called. 'And stay out of the water.'

'Okay, Mum!' they cried, as they tore away.

'Come on,' Nan said to Sarah. 'Let's find the best spot for our picnic.'

'What about over there, Nan? That looks like a good place.'

'This is lovely!' exclaimed Nan, as they inspected it. 'There are no ants and no lumps

in the ground either. What a good spotter you
are!'

Mum and Dad brought the picnic baskets
over.

'This is nice place to eat,' said Dad.

Mum rolled out a blanket for the family
to sit on. 'Where are those boys?' she
complained. 'I can't see them anywhere.'

Suddenly, SPLASH!

Everyone raced towards the water — Rene
was not a good swimmer.

A LESSON LEARNT

Rene was struggling in the water under the bridge. Dad jumped in and quickly pulled him back on to dry land.

'Are you okay?' Sarah asked her brother.

Rene nodded, but he was shaking from head to foot.

'This is a good lesson for you boys,' Nan said, after Rene had changed out of his wet clothes. 'It's easy for accidents to happen in the bush, that's why you must always stay close to your family.'

'Jay and I were just leaning over the water looking for frogs and I fell in,' Rene sniffed.

Sarah felt cross with her brothers for trying

to catch *koya* and not listening to Mum and
Nan's warnings. She wondered if the *woordatj*
had been watching them. She looked around
and saw a flash of red. Was that him?

LUNCHTIME

Everyone was so hungry after Rene's accident they decided to have an early lunch.

Soon they were tucking into the delicious damper that Nan had made the night before, as well as cold meat, salad, cheese and fruit. But they got a big surprise after their meal when a large grey kangaroo jumped up to the picnic spot and stared at them, its ears twitching.

'That's unusual,' said Dad.

Nan agreed. 'You never see *yongas* out at this time of the day.'

'Why not, Nan?' Jay asked.

'They like to rest during the day. They

make a soft spot under the trees and lay there until *kedalak* or *kedala* and then they go and look for a feed.'

'Well it's not sunset or sunrise so maybe he wants our picnic,' said Rene.

Sarah smiled. The kangaroo had cheered Rene up.

'Sometimes *yongas* run if something has scared them,' Nan said thoughtfully.

'I bet a snake frightened it,' said Jay.

Nan shook her head. 'A *yonga* would jump over a *dobitj*.'

Sarah tugged on her long brown ponytail nervously. 'Perhaps it was something short and hairy …'

Nan stood up. 'Come on,' she said. 'Let's go for a walk and see if we can find what scared that *yonga*.'

THE BUSH WALK

Sarah held Nan's hand as they wandered slowly through the bush. 'Oh, look,' she cried, 'there's a willy wagtail and he's wiggling his tail feathers.'

'*Chitty chitty* likes to tease children,' Nan said. 'It's like he's saying, "Nah, nah, nah! You can't catch me!" '

'Look what he's doing now,' said Rene.

Nan smiled. 'Yes, he's flipping and fluttering close to the ground, but as soon as we get near he'll fly off. You watch.'

Sarah stepped forward and the little bird darted away.

'Why does he do that?' asked Jay.

'It's his way of getting you to chase him,'

said Mum.

'That's right,' said Nan. 'And if you go along with his teasing, that *chitty chitty* will have you lost in the bush in no time at all. I'll tell you  children a secret: when the sand shifts in the bush, your footprints can disappear forever.'

Dad nodded in agreement. 'It's always a good idea to mark your path by leaving sticks or stones along the way. Then if the wind does blow your footprints away, you still have a trail to follow back home.'

Sarah saw Rene was looking upset again. She moved closer to him. 'What are you thinking about, Rene?'

To her surprise he burst into tears. 'I could have been lost forever! No-one would have been able to track me because you wouldn't have been able to see my footprints when I fell in the water.'

Nan gave Rene a big hug. 'If you three children listen and learn, then the *woordatj* won't come and you will always stay safe no matter where you are.'

Sarah knew this was true, but she still worried about the *woordatj*. Had that flash of red she'd seen been its eyes? Had the *woordatj* scared the *yonga*?

THE CAVE

Bending down, Sarah picked up some stones
and sticks from the ground. 'I'm going to
leave a trail behind me, like Dad said.'

'We will too,' Jay and Rene agreed.

Soon Sarah and her brothers were marking
their way through the bush. The family
walked for a long time, but they didn't see the
kangaroo again, or discover what had sent it
heading to their picnic spot.

Finally Nan stopped and looked up at the
sky. 'I think it's time to turn back. It's getting
late.'

They had gone much further than they
meant to.

As they made their way back through the bush, Sarah spotted some kangaroo poo.

'Look, *yonga goona*! Do you think it belongs to the *yonga* who visited us? Maybe he's leaving a trail too!'

Everyone laughed.

But soon, long, scary shadows began to form on the rocks around them and Nan grumbled, 'I should have kept a better eye on the time, but don't worry we'll be alright.'

They all began to walk faster, but as they drew closer to Rocky Pool, the colours of the land changed, deepening to a strange dark blue. Then Sarah spotted some more *yonga goona*, only this time it led away from the trail and towards a small cave. No-one in the family had noticed it before.

BARLAY!

'Nan!' Sarah whispered, as she halted in her tracks. 'That cave — it's just like the one you described in your story! And look, there's even a big, old, shady gum tree standing next to it.'

All of a sudden a loud noise came from deep inside the cave.

'The *woordatj*!' cried Sarah, leaping into her father's arms.

Everyone took off down the trail, but as Sarah looked back over her Dad's shoulder, she saw two long-tailed goannas scurry out the cave entrance.

'Stop!' she shouted. 'Look, it's only a pair of *karda*!'

Sarah giggled. 'I think we scared ourselves!'

'Maybe it was the goannas that spooked the *yonga*,' said Jay.

'Maybe they ran over its tail, or something!' said Rene.

Everyone laughed except Nan.

'I really think we should get going,' Nan said. 'We've stayed too long, the sun is beginning to set.'

Sarah took one final look at the cave. In the gloomy darkness two little red eyes twinkled brightly.

'*BARLAY! BARLAY!*' she cried. 'Look out! Look out! There's the *woordatj*!'

The whole family turned and fled back down the track to where their car was parked. Quickly they jumped in the station wagon and headed for home.

'Nan's story was true!' Jay said in shock.

'It wasn't a fairy story at all,' said Rene.

In her mind, Sarah could still see the red

eyes, twinkling in the dark. But they didn't seem angry. Instead it seemed to Sarah that the *woordatj* was laughing at them.

'Nan,' whispered Sarah 'I think the *woordatj* knows you're teaching us to have respect for everything that lives in the bush. Thank you for telling us about him.'

Lucky
Thamu

CHERYL KICKETT-TUCKER
AND
JAYLON TUCKER

KAARLGULA GOLDFIELDS

'Come on, Eli!' shouted Dad. 'Just throw your jocks in the bag next to your socks — that way every time you change your socks you'll remember to change your jocks as well.'

'Ahh. Don't embarrass me, Dad,' replied Eli.

Ten-year-old Eli was a Noongar-Wongi kid. His mum was a Noongar from the south-west of Western Australia and his dad was a Wongi from the north-eastern Goldfields. Eli was a gentle, shy boy with a birthmark shaped like a boomerang just above his right eye and shiny black hair down to his collar. Eli had four older brothers, two older sisters, two dogs named

Bunthar (look out) and Moorditj (solid), and a fat, fluffy ginger cat named Inni (yes).

Eli had lived in Perth all his life and often went to visit his grandparents in Kalgoorlie with his family. But these school holidays, for the first time, Eli was going by himself to visit Thamu (grandfather) and Garbarli (grandmother).

Kalgoorlie is a dusty red gold-mining town called 'kaarlgula' by the local Aboriginal people — a kaarlgula is a bush fruit, also known as the silky pear, with sweet-tasting hairy flesh. It was the best time to be in the Goldfields because it was spring. The winter rains and glorious sunshine ripened the earth into a colourful carpet of native flowers. Blue, pink, white, yellow and purple splashes of colour spread out upon the burnna yurral (red dirt) in a unique flowering explosion.

Eli liked going to his dad's hometown because he loved spending time with Thamu and Garbarli. He especially loved being spoiled by them. Garbarli made yummy chocolate mudcake just for Eli, and Thamu told him lots of yarns around the campfire at night.

Eli couldn't wait to get there, but it took all day to drive to Kalgoorlie from Perth. They arrived just before sunset.

THAMU

Thamu spoke with a soft but stern voice. He didn't have any teeth except for the false ones that he kept in a soap box — he only used the falsies when he was eating meat, otherwise he was gummy. But Thamu had the largest, smiliest smile that radiated joy to everyone. He was supposed to wear glasses but didn't and had to hold the newspaper so close that it almost touched his nose when he read. Thamu always shaved his face because if he didn't, then his grey whiskers would scratch the faces of his grannies when he gave them an oohba (kiss).

Thamu loved the smell of a campfire. He

always liked to sit in front of the flames and soak up the smoke and ash.

Thamu often said to Eli that, 'A smoky campfire is helpful when you are trying to eat food because it keeps the flies away so they don't fly into your mouth when you least expect it. It is an art to cobble together dyuwarr (dry sticks) and twigs that make the perfect simmering smoky blaze to ward away

those pesky flies.' And then Thamu would smile at him proudly, because he knew Eli was really good at building a smoky campfire.

Thamu wasn't very tall — not much taller than Eli. He was getting older but that didn't stop him from walking for miles and miles on bush trips. Thamu liked to explore in the bush and his favourite hobby was searching for unusual rocks on the ground. He especially liked to speck for gold — and sometimes he found it!

Eli wanted to be just like Thamu — strong, solid, full of knowledge, respected, proud and funny.

Eli always paid great attention when Thamu spoke because his stories helped Eli understand his part in the family and his role in looking after others, his land and his culture. Eli loved Thamu's stories because they were often shared around the campfire at night cooking yummy marshmallows.

Thamu had lots of advice about cooking marshmallows, too. 'There is a science to cooking gooey, yummy, belly-warming marshmallows,' Thamu would say. To cook a marshmallow Thamu's way, you had to find the right stick. It couldn't be green on the inside or the plant juices would cook with the mallow and you could get sick. Thamu had showed Eli how to break and tweak a stick so it was just the right length for the fire. He'd taught him to take the stick out of the fire when it started to brown and to give the mallow a blow before slipping it into his watery mouth. Mmmmmm lubbly (lovely).

THAMU'S SURPRISE

'Ahh ahh ahhhhh,' curangu (crow) echoed.
Then the other curangu started radiating the
familiar morning song to all the other crows
perched in the gum trees around Thamu's
home. Yep, you didn't need an alarm in this
place because the crows sounded long and
loud. They were worse than a rooster on a
farm because they just kept on and on and
on. 'Ahh … Ahh … Ahhhhh …'

At least a rooster would stop eventually,
thought Eli. It was so noisy he had no choice
but to roll out of bed and join Thamu.

Garbarli made some piping hot porridge.

Her cooking was always good for the soul and the stomach. Thamu had arranged a bush trip to speck for gold with Uncle Marshall, so the day ahead would be filled with adventure. Eli was so excited that even if the crows hadn't woken him, the excitement of the day would have.

Eli had just begun to drizzle sticky sweet honey on his porridge when Thamu unwrapped something from a dusty red cloth. Eli didn't take much notice, until the morning sun gleamed upon it. It almost blinded him! He jumped up from his seat in disbelief as

Thamu handed him a large chunk of gold. He nearly dropped it — although not very big, it weighed as much as ten bags of potatoes. It was as golden as butter and as smooth as steel.

'I found this gold ten years ago now,' Thamu said. 'We were camped at White Rabbit Patch — the whole family. We went hunting and I was tracking near a creek bed when I bent down to move a rock the size of my shoe. I kicked the dirt. The sun shone through and lit up the rock like a fire. I stopped and looked down … and there it was. A tiny bit of gold gleaming through the burnna yurral (red dirt).'

'What did you do, Thamu?' asked Eli.

'At first I thought it might be a small nugget, but as I dug the nugget seemed to get bigger and bigger. I dug more and more, deeper and deeper. I must have dug a hole as big as a wheelbarrow or two. It took me nearly thirty long and dusty minutes to dig it out.'

Just then, Eli heard the car crank up
as Uncle Marshall revved the engine and
shouted, 'Come on you two. There is gold to
be found!'

Uncle Marshall had already packed the car.
On the back were two jerry cans full of fresh
water — because you can't go bush without
water — some food and swags. With a rushed
oohba on Garbarli's cheek, Eli raced to the car
with Thamu right behind him.

ARE WE THERE YET?

They had been on the road for two hours
when Eli anxiously asked, 'Are we there yet?'

'Oh no, here we go,' exclaimed Uncle
Marshall. 'The famous question asked a
million times before we arrive!'

Every five minutes from then on Eli asked
again and again, 'Are we there yet?' Eli was
serious not because he was excited about
the idea of finding gold at White Rabbit, but
because Uncle Marshall was continually letting
out silent but deadly fumes. Uncle Marshall
had eaten all of the leftover marshmallows
from the night before. Thamu was not moved
by the fumigation of the car because he slept

most of the way, but Eli … Eli could take it no more.

'Let me out! Let me out!' he exclaimed. Uncle Marsh pulled the car over and the ride was complete. They arrived at White Rabbit Patch in four and a half smelly, toxic marshmallow hours.

Thamu woke when the car came to a halt. He breathed in the earthy smells of the burnna yurral. It was a familiar fragrance

and far more welcoming than the fumes from Uncle Marshall's ninjid.

Thamu opened his eyes to his favourite place. He knew every inch of this country ... the trees, waterholes, birds and animals. He was happy and excited. He had been here many, many times before. But Eli had never been to White Rabbit Patch before.

WHITE RABBIT PATCH

White Rabbit Patch was a flat area with a dry creek bed and a large waterhole at the top end of the creek. There were low shrubs and a few trees in the area — just enough vegetation and water for animals.

Thamu knew how to make the perfect camping spot. He chose a good clearing near four small trees nestled in a semicircle. Thamu broke a shrubby tree branch and used it as a broom to sweep away sticks and small rocks because Eli and Uncle Marshall would make a swag on the ground. He then instructed Uncle Marshall to park the car on the other side of the semicircle of trees to make a yor (windbreak) for the campers.

'No tents here!' Thamu said to Eli. 'The milky way is our roof, the warm breeze is our blanket and the tree is the source of our waru (fire) which will give us light.'

Eli was charged with making a campfire in the middle of the camp. It had to be a roaring fire to cook the night's meal. Thamu began to make a damper and Uncle Marshall took Eli to hunt for a marlu (kangaroo).

Dinner was over early and Eli settled down for the night with his swag in front of the campfire. 'This is the best part of the camp,' he thought as Thamu began to tell more stories of White Rabbit Patch ... like the one about the bungarra (racehorse goanna) that hides in rabbit burrows waiting for dinner to hop on in. And the one about the bungarra that creeps into your swag.

As Thamu ended his story he yelled at the top of his voice, 'Buntha (watch out)!!!!' Eli jumped in fright and hid under his swag. He

wasn't scared ... or maybe just a little. *Thamu is the greatest storyteller ever!* thought Eli as he rested his head upon his pillow and slowly closed his eyes at the milky way above.

SPECKiNG

Early in the morning, Eli woke afresh and
wriggled quickly out of his swag hoping that
a bungarra had not found a spot in his warm
bed for the night. It was the third day of the
camp. The sun was glistening, the air was
crisp. White Rabbit Patch was a very peaceful
and still place. This was Eli's country. He
was here with Thamu. Eli belonged. He was
connected ... and Thamu was proud.

For the best part of the day, Eli walked
alongside Thamu who showed him how to
speck for gold. This involved lots of walking
and looking on the ground for special rocks.
Specking was an unusual pastime but Eli really

enjoyed it because of the chance of finding something in odd spots, like under a rock or shrub. Thamu instructed Eli to search for rocks with a speck of colour in them.

'Lick the rock and tilt it so that the sun can magnify the colour.' He continued, 'If it is yellow, it could be gold. Sometimes you can speck gold in a rock but can't pick it up because it is stuck in the ground.'

Eli loved this part of specking because it involved him getting dirty and dusty. He used his very own small pick that Thamu had given him on his tenth birthday. Eli was hopeful that he could find a piece of gold that would rival Thamu's find at White Rabbit Patch.

Thamu and Eli stopped for lunch on a large mound full of rabbit holes. Eli remembered the story of the bungarra waiting for his dinner and wondered how many bungarras were in the

holes. He bent down to peer into the biggest rabbit hole he could find, when suddenly a very large white rabbit leapt out. Eli fell backwards on the burrna. He was amazed at the chance of finding a white rabbit at White Rabbit Patch!

Eli noticed that the rabbit hopped with only one foot, so he thought the rabbit would be slower and easier to catch than usual. Eli ran as fast as he could. He chased and chased and chased.

Uncle Marshall yelled to Eli, 'Fancy rabbit stew do ya, Eliiiiiiiiiii?'

Eli was a very fast runner and fancied his chances of catching the white rabbit. He was very determined. Thamu just sat and laughed and laughed at the whole fiasco.

About thirty minutes later, Eli appeared back at the camp. He was hot, sweaty, thirsty and covered in layers of red dirt. Thamu assured Eli that he had done his best to catch the rabbit, but that rabbits — especially

white ones — were
extraordinarily smart,
and out in the bush
they were considered
a sign of good luck
because they were so
rarely seen.

But to Uncle
Marshall, the white rabbit meant just one
thing — it was a sign of good myee (food).

THE FIND

That night for dinner, rabbit stew was not on the menu. The campers had kangaroo again. The excitement of rabbit chasing had wearied Eli. His eyes drooped and he dropped off to sleep watching the bright orange embers of the campfire float into the cold night and disappear as they touched the milky way.

The next morning, the campers packed up.

'There's nothing here to find this time, Eli. We best head off home,' Thamu said. Eli was still excited about the prospect of finding the white rabbit when suddenly he spotted the little critter hiding underneath a piece of warda (wood). Plates and cups were

tossed upside down as Eli scurried across
the camp with his eyes firmly fixed on that
white rabbit. Thamu and Uncle Marshall sat
in bewilderment as they had no idea what
sparked Eli's run. They didn't see the rabbit
— only Eli did. Well, he just gibbidah and was
gone in a flash across a prickly patch wearing
no shoes, just socks. Lucky for him they were
fluffy, thick socks!

The rabbit was far from the mound
where Eli had seen him the day before. The
rabbit darted here, darted there. Eli was more
determined than ever to catch that white
rabbit, especially after Thamu had told him
that they brought good luck. Eli thought to

himself that even if he touched the rabbit, then maybe the white rabbit's luck might brush onto him. Eli wanted some good luck because he was desperate to find some gold. The rabbit went down a hole. 'Aha. Got you this time,' Eli said, and waited patiently for the rabbit to come out. 'Buntha! Little rabbit, I am going to get you today,' he claimed.

After a few moments, the rabbit darted out of its hiding spot and the chase was on again. Eli lunged left, lunged right and left again but ended up face down in the burnna yurral. He stood up and wiped the dusty red earth from his face. He gave a steely stare at the rabbit who stood still for a moment and seemed to be just playing with Eli.

Again the rabbit headed for his warren. Eli remembered what Thamu had said about rabbit warrens. They were made up of lots of tunnels interconnected underground for miles and miles. Thinking he may be there for a while, he sat on a log and waited. While Eli was distracted, the smart little white rabbit pounced from the hole once again and then jolted back just as quickly, but as he did, Eli bolted from the log and gave it all he could as he exploded after the rabbit. He drew one long, deep, confident breath, reached out his arms and caught the back leg of the very fast white rabbit. A fight was on and the rabbit tossed and jumped about and leapt out of Eli's grip and out of his view.

Eli was deflated and plopped himself on the ground near the warren hole. He dropped his shoulders, sunk his head and let out a big sigh of disappointment. As soon as Eli dropped his eyes to the ground, he was

blinded by a glimmer. It took only a moment for his eyes to focus, and then he scurried across the dirt on all fours to the entrance of the rabbit warren. Eli had found good luck!

LUCKY THAMU!

Using his hands, Eli dug the rock out of the
red dirt and screamed at the top of his voice,
'Thamu, Thamu! I found it! Over here! Over
here!' It was a nugget. It was gold. It was
heavy. Thamu and Uncle Marshall raced over
in the direction of Eli's cries. They thought
that Eli had caught the white rabbit, but
soon realised that he had found gold instead.
Thamu picked up Eli and threw him in the air
in celebration.

Uncle Marshall asked, 'Where did you find
it?'

And Eli pointed to the rabbit warren.
On the road home, Eli thought about his

lucky adventure at White Rabbit Patch. He thought about the rabbit and how he had hoped it would bring him good luck. He hadn't counted on the rabbit showing him the location of a gold nugget. Eli grasped the nugget tightly in his hand as he realised he had had his lucky charm with him the whole time at White Rabbit Patch — Eli's lucky charm wasn't the rabbit or the gold. Eli's lucky charm was his Thamu.

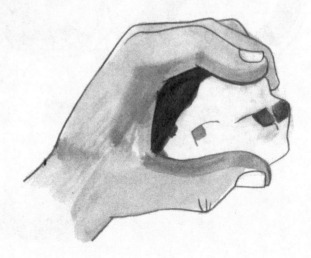

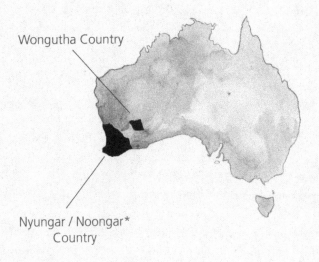

Wongutha Country

Nyungar / Noongar*
Country

*There are several accepted spellings including
Nyungar, Noongar and Nyoongar.

ABOUT THE AUTHORS

Tjalaminu Mia was born in Perth in 1952. Her
people are the Menang and Goreng Nyungar
people. Her country is Nyungar country, which
covers a large part of the south-west of Western
Australia. The languages of her people are
Nyungar and English.

When she was young, she loved the stories
her grandfather told her about their culture,
especially the stories about the birds and
the Emu man. Her stories are inspired by the
wonderful and exciting things he showed her
that grew and lived in the bush when she was a
little girl.

Jessica Lister was born in 1992, and her country is Nyungar country, too.

Jessica likes drawing and listening to music. Her favourite places are the bush in the hills outside of Perth, the beach and the town of Albany.

Jessica really enjoyed writing this story with her grandmother. She says, 'Nan talked to me about the special times when she was growing up, which were real *mooditj* — good!'

Cheryl Kickett-Tucker belongs to three groups of the Noongar people — Wadjuk (Swan River), Balladong (Wheatbelt) and Yued (Moora). Cheryl was born in Wadjuk country in Subiaco and grew up in Lockridge and Midland. She loves going bush with her family and she especially loves the adventures they have when going to the Goldfields. There is lots to explore and lots to learn about 'country'.

Barlay was inspired by the tales she tells her own children and by the legends her mother passed onto her. She wanted to write a Noongar tale so that all kids, particularly Noongar kids, could share in Noongar legends about country and culture.

Lucky Thamu comes from Wongutha country in the Goldfields and is based on a mix of true stories about Thamu, to whom this book is dedicated.

Jaylon Tucker identifies as a Wongi-Noongar. He was born on Wadjuk Noongar country. Through his father he also belongs to the Ngullundharra and Walyan Aboriginal people of Wongutha country in the north-east Western Australian Goldfields.

Jaylon spent a lot of time with his Thamu and has enjoyed going bush to explore. He really loves going camping and making fires, hunting and sleeping under the stars. He also loves the stories that Thamu has told him over the years.

Lucky Thamu is based on a series of events that he has shared with his Thamu and the adventures of gold hunting.

LIKE THESE STORIES?
TRY:

AVAILABLE NOW